MARVEL

THE MIGHTY THOR

AN ORIGIN STORY

Based on the Marvel comic book series **Thor**
Adapted by **Rich Thomas**
Interior illustrated by **The Storybook Art Group**
Cover illustrated by **Pat Olliffe** and **Brian Miller**

Bath • New York • Singapore • Hong Kong • Cologne • Delhi
Melbourne • Amsterdam • Johannesburg • Auckland • Shenzhen

First published by Parragon in 2012

Parragon
Queen Street House
4 Queen Street
Bath BA1 1HE, UK
www.parragon.com

www.marvel.com

™ & © 2012 Marvel & Subs.

ISBN 978-1-4454-5984-4

Printed in China

What would it be like to live among **legends**? To be something **more** than human?

To hold **great power** in your hands...

and know how to **use** it?

To be **feared**?

To be **brave**,

to be **honoured** –

to be **MIGHTY**?

Some are **born** with these qualities.

And some spend their lives **working** to attain them.

This is a story about someone who was born into royalty, **but needed to earn his honour**.

This is a story about a **hero**...

named **THOR**.

Thor's realm was called **Asgard**.
It sat like an island whose shores
were swept by the sea of space.

The people who lived on Asgard were
called **Asgardians** and the Asgardians
called our world **Midgard**. The only way
to reach our world from theirs was by the
rainbow bridge, **Bifrost**. The bridge was
guarded by the sentry called **Heimdall**.

Even though Asgard was well protected,
threats were endless.

Thor was one of the land's **great
protectors**.

He was also a prince. He lived with his brother Loki in the castle of their father, Odin.

Thor was arrogant and chose his friends for their loyalty: the brave warrior Balder, and a band of soldiers called the Warriors Three – Fandral, Volstagg and Hogun – and the beautiful, strong and wise Lady Sif.

Thor's father, Odin, ruled over all of Asgard.

He and his wife, Frigga, wanted nothing
more than for their sons to grow up to
be worthy rulers.

But there could only be one supreme ruler of Asgard.
Only one who could be like Odin. And even though
Loki was thoughtful, clever and quick...

Thor was **first born**, and so the throne was his by right.

To determine when Thor would be ready to rule, Odin had a special hammer made. It was forged from a mystical metal called **Uru**, which came from the heart of a dying star.

The hammer was named...
Mjolnir, and it held
great power.

But no one would be able to lift the hammer unless he or she was **worthy**.

The hammer was **immovable** to Thor.

Still, Odin's actions made it clear:
The hammer was meant for his
first born son and no one else.

Even so, proving worthy of Mjolnir was not an easy task.

Thor spent nearly every moment trying to earn his right to hold the hammer. He performed amazing acts of **bravery**,

he was honoured
for acts of **nobility**...

and he demonstrated
feats of great **strength**...

and **honour**.

With every great achievement, Thor attempted once more to pick up Mjolnir. It seemed as if he would never raise the hammer more than a few inches from the table.

And then
one day...

he DID.

Thor had proven himself worthy
of his weapon, and he used it well.
When he threw the hammer, it
always returned to him.

When he twirled it by its handle,
he could soar like a winged beast!

**And when he slammed it
twice upon the ground...**

he could summon all the power of
lightning, **rain** and **thunder**!

In fact, with his hammer in hand,
there was little Thor could not do.

And he knew it.

Odin wanted him to be a great warrior, and he had become one. His father wanted him to earn the respect of Asgard. He had it. But then Thor began to let the power go to his head.

And Odin was not happy.

In fact, he had grown quite angry with his son.

Odin called Thor to his throne room. Thor knew that **something was wrong**. His father rarely summoned him in such a harsh tone. Thor was sure that his **jealous brother** Loki had spun some **lie** to get him into trouble.

But nothing could have been further from Thor's mind than what Odin had to say to him.

Odin told Thor that he was his **favoured son.**

He told him that he was brave beyond compare and noble as a prince must be.

He told him that his **strength** was **legendary** and that he was the **best warrior** in the kingdom.

But Thor did not know what it meant to be **weak** or to feel **pain**. And without knowing **humility**, Thor could never be a truly **honourable** warrior.

Odin was angry. In his rage, he tore Mjolnir from Thor's hand and threw it toward Midgard. Then he stripped Thor of his armour and sent him to Earth.

Odin made his son believe that he was a medical student with an injured leg, named **Don Blake**.

As Blake, Thor learned to **study hard**. At times he thought he might **fail**. But he worked harder than he ever had in Asgard, and in the end he **earned** his degree.

He allowed others to **help** him with his injury. In doing so, he discovered that people were generally **good**. Thor learned to truly love humanity. As a surgeon, he **treated the sick**.

He helped **weak** people find their **strengths**.

And one day, while on holiday in Norway...

Don Blake found himself trapped in a cave.
The only possible exit lay behind a boulder.

He found a staff on the ground and shoved it under the boulder. He tried with all his might to move the rock. He pushed and pushed.

Nothing.

He was so angry that he took the staff and **struck** it on the ground. And that's when it became clear that it was no ordinary stick.

It was **Mjolnir** in disguise!

Odin had sent Don to this cave. Odin, the All Father of Asgard, was **pleased**.

His son had learned **humility**.

He had at long last become a complete **hero**.

He had become **human in spirit**, but still, now and forever...

he was
THE MIGHTY THOR.